To my mum, and to the spirit of her three dachshunds
in Hound Heaven: Chanda, Sano and Chota
P. B.

To Harry and Joe
T. M.

First published in 2016 by Scholastic Children's Books
Euston House, 24 Eversholt Street
London NW1 1DB
a division of Scholastic Ltd
www.scholastic.co.uk
London ~ New York ~ Toronto ~ Sydney ~ Auckland
Mexico City ~ New Delhi ~ Hong Kong

Text copyright © 2016 Peter Bently
Illustrations copyright © 2016 Tom McLaughlin

ISBN 978 1407 14567 9

1 3 5 7 9 10 8 6 4 2

The moral rights of Peter Bently and Tom McLaughlin have been asserted.

Papers used by Scholastic Children's Books are made from wood grown in sustainable forests.

HOT DOG
HAL

Peter Bently * Tom McLaughlin

SCHOLASTIC

Hal loved his blanket.
There's no doubt about it.
He wore it all day and went nowhere without it.

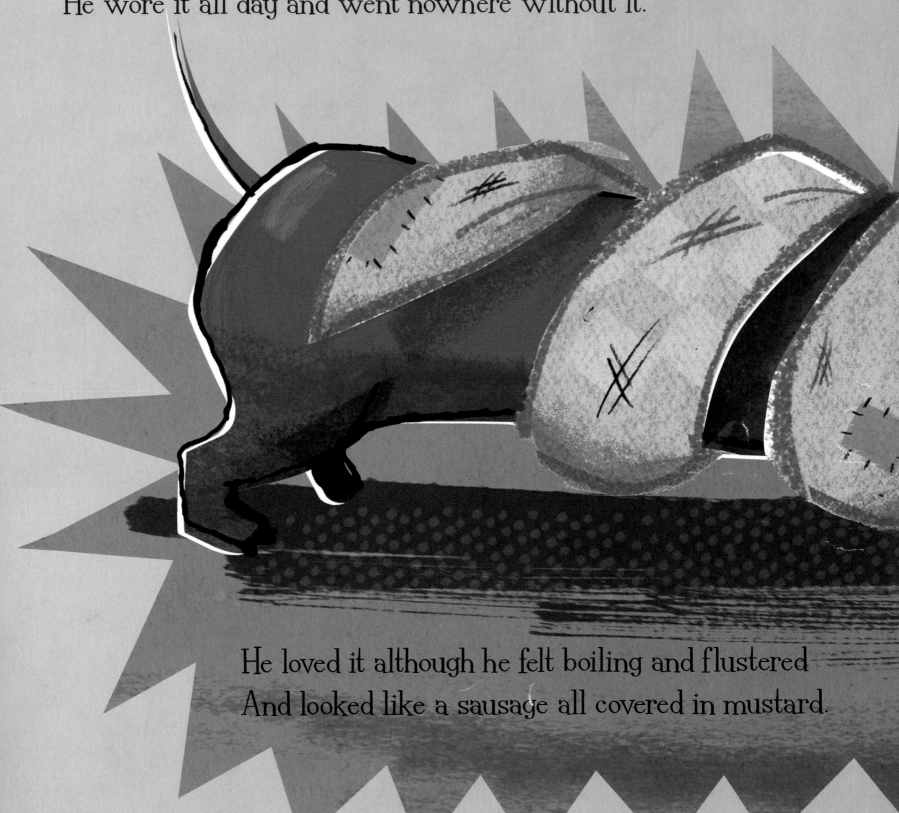

He loved it although he felt boiling and flustered
And looked like a sausage all covered in mustard.

"In fact," chuckled
Buster McNally, his pal,
"From now on I'm calling you

Hot
DOG
HAL!"

Hal wore his blanket for strolling and chasing.

He wore it for catching...

...and snatching...

...and racing.

He wore it for digging up big tasty bones
With Buster and Tootsie and young Nipper Jones.

"Hey, **Hot Dog**," said Buster,
   "You look like you're stewing!"
"I'm fine," panted Hal,
   as he carried on chewing.

"I've had this old blanket since I was a pup.
I know it's too hot but I won't give it up!"

Hal wore his blanket
for trips to the zoo.

If he went to the **seaside** along it went too.
The blanket made Hal feel exceedingly hot.
But would he remove it? Most certainly not.

It made all the other dogs giggle and scoff,
But in spite of the heat he would NOT take it off.
"It's cosy and cuddly and snuggly as well
And it has a nice biscuity chocolatey smell."

"A blanket," said Tootsie,
    "belongs on a bed."
"A blanket? Oh no.
    It's...a hammock," Hal said.

"It's a Halloween costume,
    a ghostly disguise –
It's even got two little holes
    for my eyes!

It's a sail!

It's a house!

It's a cape!

It's a flag!"

"Don't be daft," chuckled Nipper. "It's just an old rag!"

"Never mind, **Hot Dog**," grinned Buster McNally,
"Come and play hide-and-seek down in the alley."

While Buster was counting it started to rain,
So they ran to the windmill in Ticklemore Lane.

The weather grew worse
as they fled helter skelter
Up the rickety staircase
and into their shelter.

They huddled inside. It was really quite frightening
As the old windmill shook in the thunder and lightning.

"Come under my blanket, it's lovely and warm!"
Said Hal, "It'll make you feel safe from the storm."
His friends snuggled under and had to agree
That the blanket was rather a nice place to be.

Then the pooches all yelped as the lightning went FLASH!
And the thunder went BOOM!

and then *something* went

CRASH!

"Yikes! What was that?" wondered Hal with a frown.

"The staircase!" cried Buster.
"It's just fallen down!"

"Oh no!" fretted Nipper.
"What terrible luck!
We're trapped in the windmill!"
he whimpered. "We're stuck!"

"If only," cried Tootsie,
"we had a long rope!"
And suddenly Hal
felt a glimmer of hope.

"We don't have a rope,
that's for certain," he said.
"So we'll just have to use
my old **blanket** instead!"

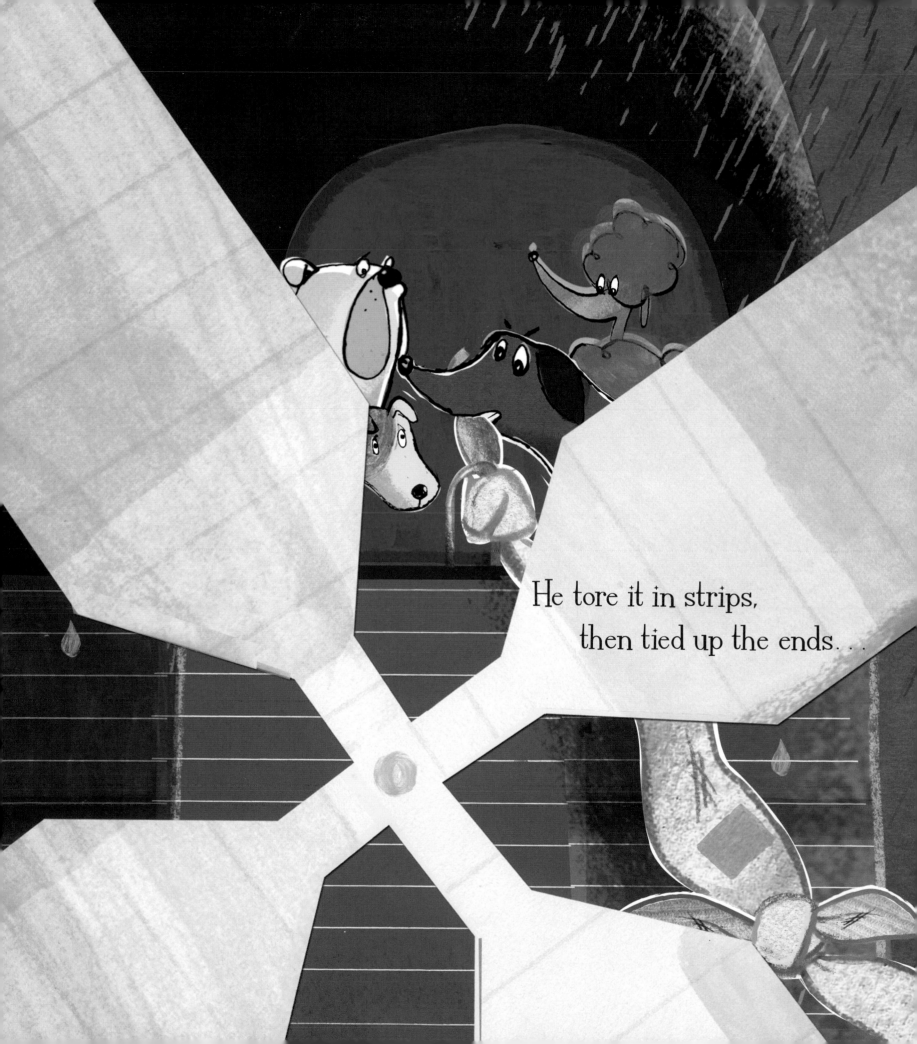

He tore it in strips,
then tied up the ends....

And ...climbed

down

to safety

with all of his friends.

Said Buster and Nipper, "I'm sorry we laughed.
I'm sorry we said that your blanket was daft."

"But I can't go on wearing it now,"
Hal said sadly.
"It's torn and it's battered
and tattered so badly."

Then Buster grinned.
"I've an idea," he said.
"We just need some scissors,
a needle, and thread."

Now Hal and his friends
go to play in the alley
In their trendy new shirts
made by Buster McNally.

On one side of Hal's it says. . .

SAUSAGE
DOGS
RULE!

But his **friends**
all have shirts that say...

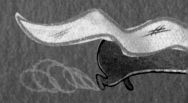